Disney's

TOY STORY

A FRIEND IS...

MOUSE WORKS

A friend is...

someone you like to spend time with.

A friend is...

someone who is loyal.

A friend is...

someone who always knows how you feel.

A friend is...

someone who makes you laugh.

A friend is...

someone who is always happy to see you.

A friend is...

someone who helps you see things clearly.

A friend is...

someone who looks out for you.

A friend is...

someone who won't repeat what you tell him.

A friend is...

someone who makes you feel good about yourself.

A friend is a friend...

to infinity and beyond!